CANNONBALL CORALIE AND THE LION

THIS BOOK BELONGS TO:

....

FOR MUM and DAD
WHO FILLED MY LIFE WITH BOOKS
AND FOR OSCAR
WHO PREFERS LOOKING AT THE PICTURES

First published in 2018 by Lincoln Children's Books
First published in paperback in 2018 by Lincoln Children's Books,
an imprint of The Quarto Group.
The Old Brewery, 6 Blundell Street, London N7 9BH, United Kingdom.
T (0)20 7700 6700 F (0)20 7700 8066 www.QuartoKnows.com

A catalogue record for this book is available from the British Library.
ISBN 978-1-78603-700-8
The illustrations were created digitally.
Handlettered and set in Futura
Published by Katie Cotton
Commissioned by Jenny Broom
Designed by Zoë Tucker
Edited by Kate Davies
Production by Jenny Cundill and Kate O'Riordan
Manufactured in Guangdong, China TL082018

1 3 5 7 9 8 6 4 2

CANNONBALL CORALIE AND THE LION

Lincoln Children's
First Editions

There was a little girl who lived in the woods, who didn't like rules. Her name was Coralie.

She could swing from tree to tree,

and juggle five squirrels at a time,

and stand on her hands.

She was funny and brave
and silly and strange.

But no one was there to see her.

Until one day, marching through the woods came acrobats
and trumpeters, drummers and jugglers, and best of all…

A LION!

They seemed loud and brave and exciting and odd – a lot like Coralie. Coralie decided to follow them.

They arrived at a place Coralie had never seen before, full of lights and colours and daring tricks. And there, in the middle of it all, was the lion.

Coralie thought he was wonderful.

'ROAR!'

said Lion, which meant,
'Would you like to play with me?
We could do tricks together.
If we're allowed...'

And Coralie said, 'Yes, please.'

She found a man in a big hat, who was telling everyone what to do.

'LESS WOBBLING!'

'MORE BANANAS!'

'AND ABSOLUTELY NO JAZZ!' he shouted.

He looked in charge, so Coralie asked, 'Please can I stay here with you all? I may be small but I can do all sorts of tricks. And I would like to be friends with your lion.'

The Man in the Big Hat looked at her and said,

'WE DON'T HAVE FRIENDS HERE, BUT LET ME SEE WHAT YOU CAN DO.'

Coralie could balance
very high,

and juggle
cats and dogs,

and pull rabbits out of hats.

'ROAR!' said Lion, which meant, 'You are very talented, for a human so small!'

But the Man in the Big Hat was not impressed. 'Your tricks are not good enough,' he said. 'But you are just the right size to be...'

'... A HUMAN CANNONBALL!'

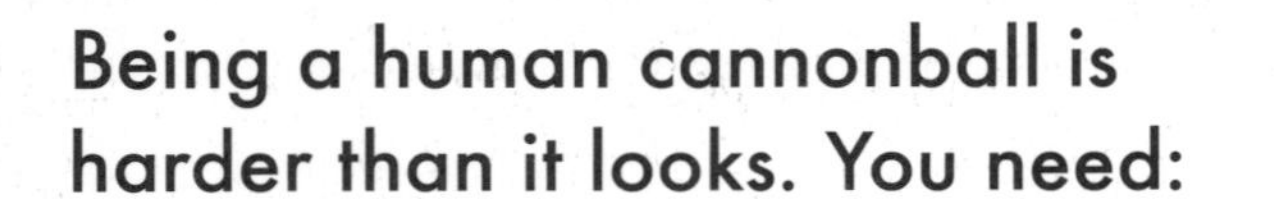

Being a human cannonball is harder than it looks. You need:

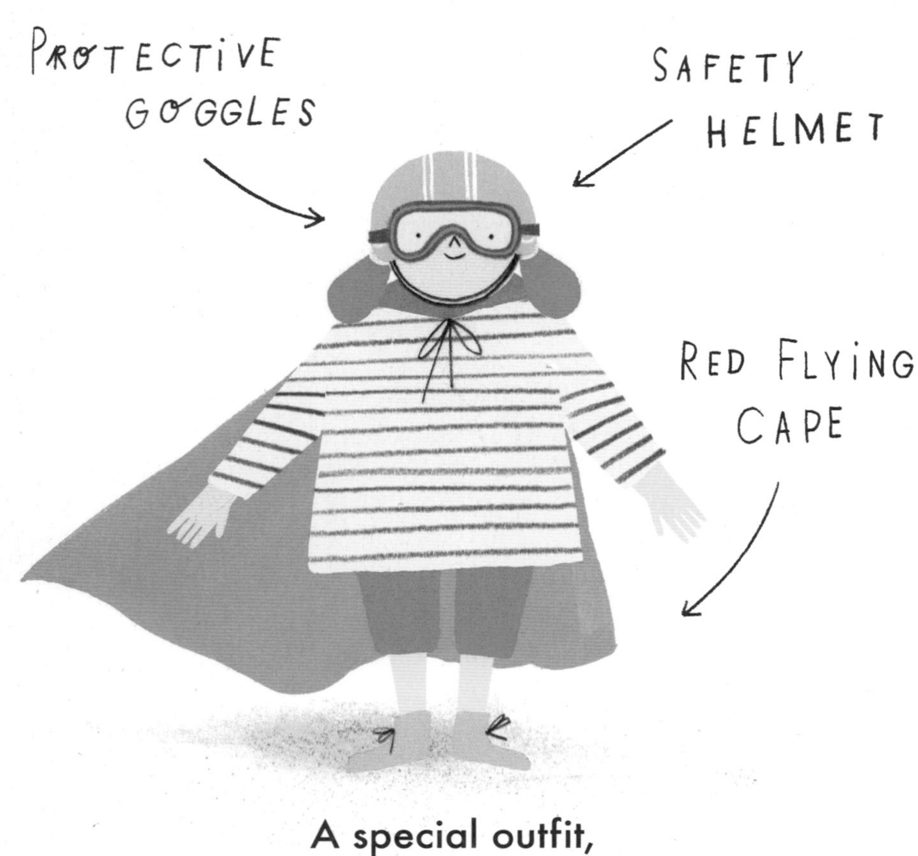

A special outfit,

an impressive flying pose,

and most importantly, to be extremely brave.

Coralie was extremely brave.
But the cannon was extremely tall.
'What if I can't do it?' said Coralie.

'ROAR!'

said Lion, which meant,
'I think you can do anything!'

That night, Coralie stroked Lion for luck.
As she climbed into the cannon, the jugglers
and acrobats and trumpeters all held their breath.

Coralie shut her eyes tight,
held her chin to the sky and then...

KABOOM!

The crowd hollered and clapped and whooped and cheered! Coralie felt as though she might explode with happiness.

ROAR!

said Lion, which meant, 'You were amazing!'

But the Man in the Big Hat didn't look happy at all.

'YOUR ARMS WEREN'T STRAIGHT,
YOU DIDN'T POINT YOUR TOES,
YOUR LANDING WAS FLOPPY AND
YOU DIDN'T DO A SINGLE SOMERSAULT.

PACK YOUR BAGS AND

GO!'

Coralie didn't have any bags to pack, but
she did have someone to say goodbye to.
'I'll miss you,' she said to Lion, and she
hugged him very tight.

Lion started to follow Coralie – but then the Man in the Big Hat appeared, and shouted:

'GET BACK TO WORK!
MORE TRICKS!
LESS SMILING!
AND ABSOLUTELY
NO CARING ABOUT
EACH OTHER!'

Lion looked at the Man in the Big Hat
– and so much anger and sadness swelled up
inside him that he let out a loud, lonely...

This time it didn't mean anything.
Sometimes a roar is just a roar.

The roar was so loud and so long and
so lonely that it blew the man
and his big hat far, far away.

Coralie heard Lion's roar echo through the trees. 'I can't leave my friend behind,' she thought. She turned back to find him,

and there, walking away from the circus, came acrobats and trumpeters, drummers and jugglers, and best of all...

...Lion.

'ROAR!'

said Lion, which meant 'We're free at last!
Can we stay here with you?'

And Coralie hugged him, which meant, 'Of course.'

Now there's a group of friends
who live in the woods,
who don't like rules.

They swing through the trees,

and stand on their hands,

and juggle five squirrels at
a time – just for fun.

And every night, when the stars come out,
Coralie gives Lion a goodnight hug.
'I love you,' she says.
And Lion says...

'ROAR!'
Which means, 'I love you, too.'

HAVE YOU READ THESE OTHER TITLES FROM LINCOLN CHILDREN'S FIRST EDITIONS?

The Best Sound in the World

Cindy Wume

ISBN: 978-1-78603-169-3

Roy is a lion and a sound catcher. Trying to avoid his irritating neighbour Jemmy, he goes on a hunt for the best sound in the world. He travels far and wide to no avail... can Roy realise that perhaps friendship is the best thing of all?

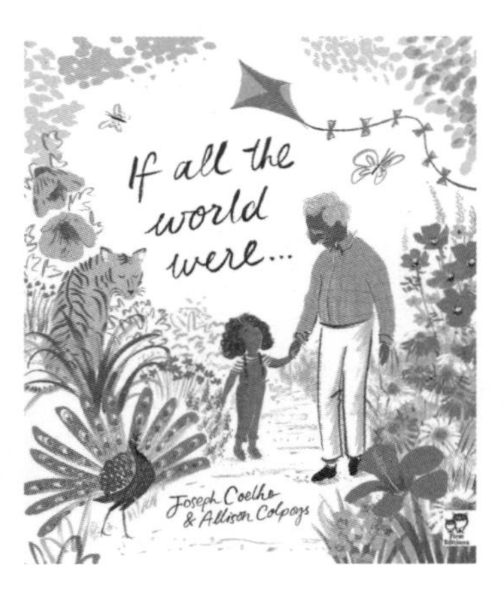

If All the World Were...

Joseph Coelho and Alison Colpoys

ISBN: 978-1-78603-059-7

Grandad gives me a pencil with a rainbow nib. "Write and draw, write and draw all your dreams." A moving picture book about a girl's love for her granddad and how, through memories, love can live on.

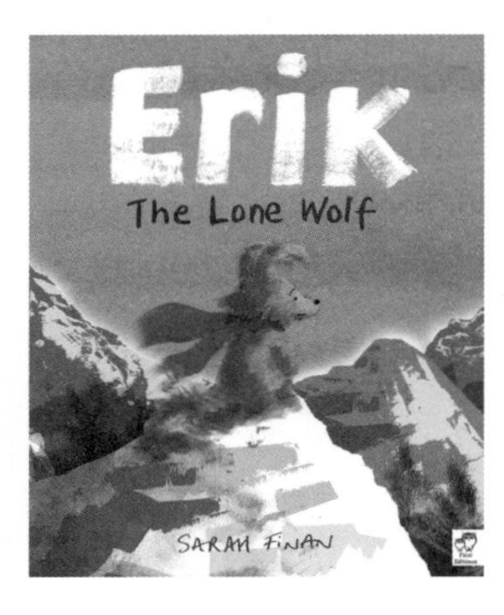

Erik the Lone Wolf

Sarah Finan

ISBN: 978-1-78603-010-8

Being a wolf means sticking with the pack. Everyone knows that – except for Erik, one little wolf cub who dreams of setting off on his own adventure...all by himself! But will life as a lone wolf be everything he hoped, or will he miss the rough and tumble of the pack?

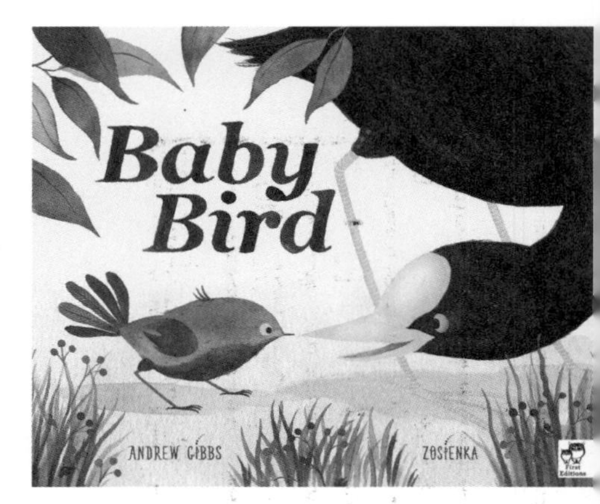

Baby Bird

Andrew Gibbs and Zosienka

ISBN: 978-1-78603-012-2

'All birds are born to fly,' thinks Baby Bird, watching the other hatchlings leave the nest. 'I suppose it's now or never...' But one of Baby's wings is twisted and shrunken and not at all like the other one. Instead of flying, Baby plummets to the ground. There, Baby makes a new friend, and learns that sometimes you have to find unexpected ways to achieve your dreams.

Lincoln Children's First Editions